W9-BLK-355

# Keller's Heart

BY
## John Gray

ILLUSTRATED BY
## Shanna Brickell

PARACLETE PRESS
BREWSTER, MASSACHUSETTS

2019 First Printing
*Keller's Heart*

Text copyright © 2019 by John Gray
Illustrations copyright © 2019 by Shanna Obelenus

ISBN 978-1-64060-174-1

The Paraclete Press name and logo (dove on cross) are trademarks of Paraclete Press, Inc.

Library of Congress Cataloging-in-Publication Data

Names: Gray, John Joseph, 1962- author. | Brickell, Shanna, illustrator.
Title: Keller's heart / by John Gray ; illustrated by Shanna Brickell.
Description: Brewster, Massachusetts : Paraclete Press, 2019. | Series: All
  god's creatures | Summary: Raven, a girl who is deaf, adopts a blind and
  deaf puppy and together they encourage others to judge not by what they
  see, but rather by what is within.
Identifiers: LCCN 2018044803 | ISBN 9781640601741 (hardback)
Subjects: | CYAC: Deaf—Fiction. | People with disabilities—Fiction. |
  Dogs—Fiction. | Animals with disabilities—Fiction. | Animal
  rescue—Fiction. | BISAC: RELIGION / Christian Life / Family. | JUVENILE
  FICTION / Religious / Christian / Animals. | JUVENILE FICTION / Religious
  / Christian / Social Issues. | JUVENILE FICTION / Social Issues / Special
  Needs. | JUVENILE FICTION / Animals / Dogs.
Classification: LCC PZ7.1.G733 Kel 2019 | DDC [E]—dc23
LC record available at https://lccn.loc.gov/2018044803

10 9 8 7 6 5 4 3 2 1

Published by Paraclete Press
Brewster, Massachusetts
www.paracletepress.com

Printed in The United States of America

*F*or any child who has ever felt different,
alone, or faced special challenges.
You are unique.
You are beautiful.
You are loved.

$\mathcal{T}$his is a love story, but not the kind with castles, dragons, and a princess trapped in a tower. It does, however, have a special girl and a fluffy knight who rescue each other.

The little girl's name was Raven, and she had a lot to say for someone who never spoke. She was as quiet as a butterfly dancing on a cloud. You see, Raven was deaf. She talked with her hands, her smile, her hugs. She gave the best hugs. Raven was excited because it was almost her birthday.

On the other side of town was Raven's
best friend who she hadn't met yet: a puppy
without a name or home or a child to love.
This puppy was different. He couldn't see or
hear, but his nose was extra-sensitive and his
heart was as big as the sky.

Sometimes when things appear broken people throw them away or think they aren't as good— but that's not true. Sometimes, different is better.

Yet, when this puppy's owner saw that the puppy's eyes and ears didn't work, he left him on the side of the road near the train tracks and drove off. The owner didn't realize it, then, but he'd just thrown away the most precious thing a person could ever have—a friend.

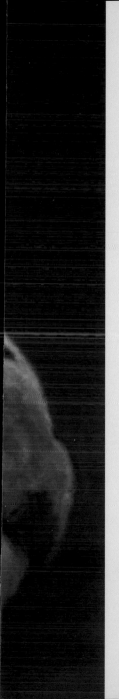

The puppy's hair grew long, and he got very dirty wandering the streets. Then one day a nice lady found him and took him to the animal shelter. He needed a name, a home, and especially a bath.

Even though Raven was deaf she did all the things other children did at school, only she had an aide to help her communicate with her classmates. Raven taught them simple sign language like "hello" and "how are you?", but she got lonely sometimes being the only one like her at school. Plus, some of the kids treated her differently, as if she would break if they played with her. She was deaf, not made of glass. Raven just wanted to fit in.

One day her class took a field trip to the animal shelter. They had a tour and saw furry creatures big and small. As everyone crowded around a box of kittens, Raven's eyes were drawn to a back room and the sight of water splashing.

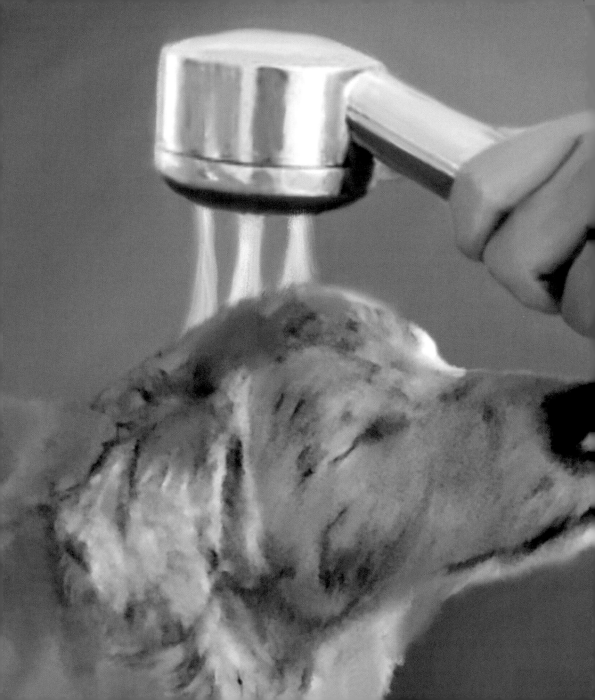

She walked over and saw they were washing the puppy that was found by the train tracks. Soon, the other children joined her, but they couldn't see what Raven could see. The puppy didn't have his eyes closed because of the soap; they were closed because he was blind.

She noticed something else, too. On the puppy's left side was a big dark spot. They scrubbed it and scrubbed it but it didn't come clean.

When the bath was done, they dried him off, and the puppy raised his nose in the air. He could tell there were lots of people in the room now, and he was sniffing them all without moving a single step. Then he lowered his nose and, of all the children in the room, he walked directly over to Raven and rested his head on her foot.

"He likes you," the worker said. "You wanna give him a drink? He can't see and hear so you have to help him."

Raven took the bowl of water and got on the floor with the puppy. Rather than give him a drink immediately, she took his left paw and tapped it twice in her hand, then gave him a sip. She did this a second and third time, and soon the dog wagged his tail anticipating what would come next.

"What's she doing?" her classmate asked. The teacher smiled and said, "Teaching him doggie sign language."

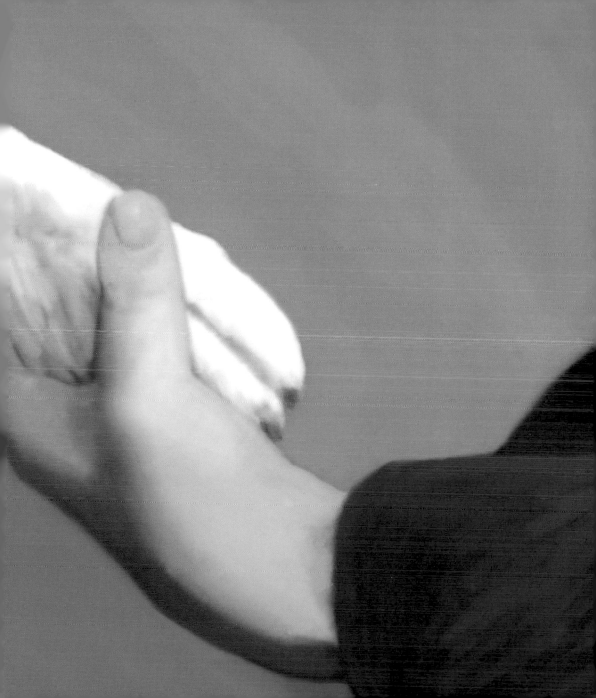

When Raven went home she told her parents what she wanted for her birthday, and the next day the puppy without a name was hers.

Raven had recently read a book about an amazing woman named Helen Keller who was deaf and blind – so she called the puppy Keller.

Over the next few months, Raven taught Keller more sign language, and with her mom's permission, she took him to the children's hospital to visit. Raven thought that if the sick kids saw how well she and her puppy were doing, this would inspire them and show them it is OK to be different.

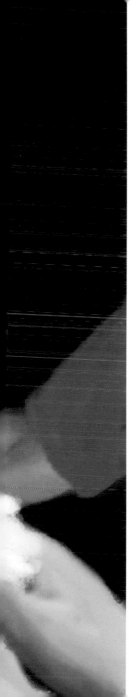

Soon she was taking him to nursing homes and other hospitals for more smiles.

For a dog trapped in darkness, Keller was full of light.

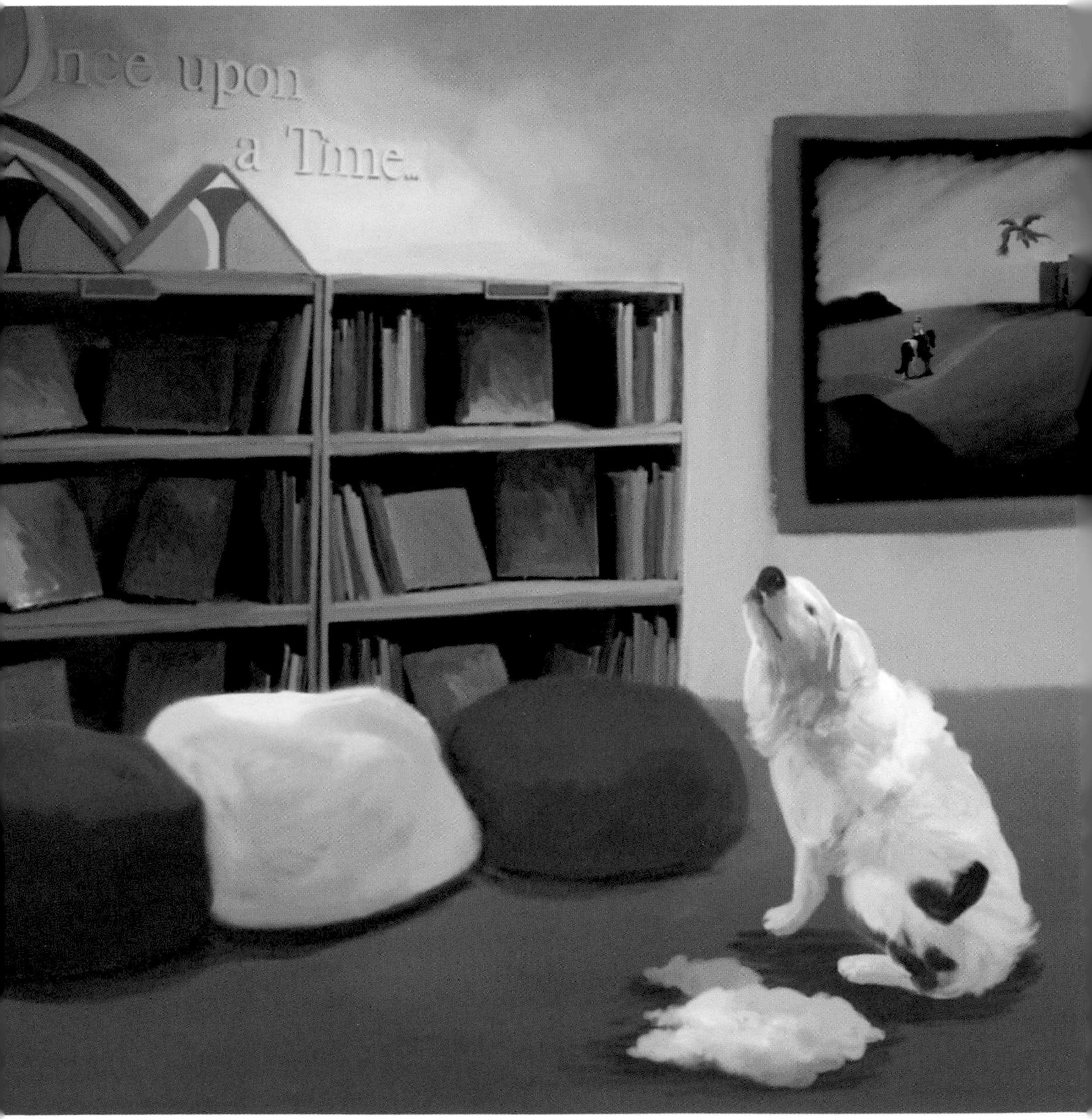
Once upon
a Time...

On the last day of school, Raven's teacher let her bring Keller to class for Show and Tell, but she wasn't alone. "Is this your mom?" they asked. "No" she signed, "It's a groomer. Watch this." Raven smiled, knowing what was about to happen.

The woman took out scissors and started trimming back Keller's fur, especially that dark spot on his left side. Soon they saw that, hidden underneath the tangled mess in his fur, was a perfectly shaped heart.

Raven showed them not to judge people by what they see. It is what's underneath and inside that counts.

She then signed to the class, "This is Keller. I am his eyes and he is my heart."

The quietest girl at school revealed the most important lesson of all. It was right there in Keller's heart.

❤

John Norton Photography

*Hi,*

My name is Keller—the REAL Keller who inspired this story. I'm so glad you came by to visit with me.

Just like the puppy in the book, I was born unable to see and hear, and someone left me on the side of the road. Then something AMAZING happened. A nice family adopted me from the shelter, and I went to live with them.

Now I get hugs and kisses every day, and I have other puppies to play with. I really do have a big ❤ in my fur. I even have one on my paw.

I love the snow and playing in the leaves too. Even though I'm different from other dogs, I've learned to never give up. Don't you give up either.

Remember, you're special just the way you are. Bye!!!

*Keller*